The Great Silent Grandmother Gathering

The Great Silent Grandmother Gathering

A Story for Anyone Who Thinks
She Can't Save the World

SHARON MEHDI

Viking

VIKING
Published by the Penguin Group
Penguin Group (USA) Inc., 375 Hudson Street, New York, New York 10014, U.S.A. • Penguin
Group (Canada), 10 Alcorn Avenue, Toronto, Ontario, Canada M4V 3B2 (a division of Pearson Pen-
guin Canada Inc.) • Penguin Books Ltd, 80 Strand, London WC2R 0RL, England • Penguin Ire-
land, 25 St. Stephen's Green, Dublin 2, Ireland (a division of Penguin Books Ltd) • Penguin Books
Australia Ltd, 250 Camberwell Road, Camberwell, Victoria 3124, Australia (a division of Pearson
Australia Group Pty Ltd) • Penguin Books India Pvt Ltd, 11 Community Centre, Panchsheel Park,
New Delhi – 110 017, India • Penguin Group (NZ), Cnr Airborne and Rosedale Roads, Albany,
Auckland 1310, New Zealand (a division of Pearson New Zealand Ltd) • Penguin Books (South
Africa) (Pty) Ltd, 24 Sturdee Avenue, Rosebank, Johannesburg 2196, South Africa

Penguin Books Ltd, Registered Offices: 80 Strand, London WC2R 0RL, England

This edition first published in 2005 by Viking Penguin, a member of Penguin Group (USA) Inc.

10 9 8 7 6 5 4 3 2 1

PUBLISHER'S NOTE
This is a work of fiction. Names, characters, places, and incidents either are the product of the au-
thor's imagination or are used fictitiously, and any resemblance to actual persons, living or dead,
business establishments, events, or locales is entirely coincidental.

CIP data available.
ISBN 0–670–03460–6

This book is printed on acid-free paper. ∞

Printed in Mexico

Illustrations by Ellen Anderson

Designed by Carla Bolte • Set in Garamond

For Laila and her great-grandmother

♡

Sunday

On a buffety, blustery early summer day, when the news was bad and the sky turned yellow, a strange thing happened in the town where I live. That morning, two grandmothers who had never met, not even by accident, put on their summer Sunday clothes, their most comfortable shoes, their favorite sun hats, and walked to the park in the center of town.

Now that, of course, wasn't the strange part because lots of people walk to the park, especially in summer.

It's what the grandmothers did after they got there that set the whole town on its collective ear.

What, you ask, could two grandmothers do that would cause such a buzz on a buffety, blustery early summer day? Well, just wait till you hear.

The grandmothers who had never met, not even by accident, walked past the river and past the rose garden and past the playground to the center of the big grassy area that faces the town square. And there they stood.

Not speaking.

Not looking at squirrels.

Not munching on coconut candy.

In actual point of fact, *not anything at all.*

Ryan Reilly was the first to notice. He's the busboy at Beever Brothers Café that overlooks the park. Every time he cleared coffee cups and water glasses from the table by the window, he saw the grandmothers.

"What do you think they're doing?" he asked Willie and Erma Beans, who always sit at the table by the window.

"Dunno," said Willie.

"Maybe they're waiting for someone," Erma offered.

"Mighty long wait," said Ryan.

Robin the waitress bustled by with a coffeepot. "Maybe they're pretending to be statues," she said. "People do that, you know."

Sue Ann Renfrew got up and looked out the window. "Maybe it's a Chinese meditation exercise."

"Well, if that's exercise, it's the kind I could get into," said Leslie Plunkett, who, with her five-year-old daughter, Polly, joined Sue Ann at the window.

For several minutes everyone in Beever Brothers Café watched the grandmothers stand in the center of the big grassy area. No one could come up with a reasonable explanation for their behavior. No one, that is, until a very little voice said, "I know what they're doing." Leslie looked down at her topsy-haired daughter.

"You do?" said Willie and Erma and Sue Ann and Leslie and Ryan Reilly and Robin the waitress.

"Yes," she said, suddenly shy from all the attention.

"Well then tell us," said Ryan Reilly.

Polly took a gulpy breath and announced quite matter-of-factly, as a matter of fact: "They're saving the world."

For exactly two-point-five seconds, no one said a word. Then they all laughed. Leslie scooped up her daughter and everyone went back to their tables, and that was that.

Except it wasn't.

When Ryan Reilly got off work that afternoon, he cut through the park on his way home like he always does, and the grandmothers were still there. They had been standing in the middle of the big grassy area the whole day long.

Ryan was puzzled, perplexed and more than a little perturbed. The world was already askew and getting askewer every day. If grandmothers started doing unpredictably curious things, there was no telling where it might end. At that very moment, more than anything, he needed to know why they were standing in the park.

So he did the only thing he could think of—he asked.

The grandmothers, whose glistening faces were as pink as watermelon flesh, smiled weary smiles. And with just a hint of sadness, mixed with just a hint of hope, they said almost in unison: "We're saving the world."

This was definitely *not* what Ryan wanted to hear. It made no sense. Two grandmothers standing in the park can't save the world. Everyone knows that—except maybe Polly Plunkett, but she's only five.

He didn't know what to say next, and the more he didn't know what to say, the more flustered he got. "It's just that . . . well . . . you can't . . ." Finally, he threw his hands in the air and darted across the lawn toward home, his face as pink as the grandmothers'.

∞

The big television set in the family room was on when Ryan and his parents sat down to dinner. They always ate with the TV turned to the news, and the news was always bad. Lately it had been especially bad.

The only time anyone talked during dinner, except to say, "Please pass the parsnips," was when a commercial came on. That night, Ryan could hardly wait for the commercial so he could tell his parents about the two grandmothers who stood in the park all day.

"Why would they do such a thing?" asked his mother.

"They said they're saving the world."

His father laughed, shook his head and kept on eating. But his mother stopped, a fork full of parsnips suspended in the air midway between the plate and her mouth. She stared at her son, saying nothing, even though the commercial was still on and it was okay to talk.

That same evening, Willie and Erma Beans met with their weekly cribbage-and-dessert group. Erma told the women at her table about the grandmothers who stood in the park doing nothing.

When Madeline Swivet asked, "Whatever for?" Erma said, "I heard they're saving the world." She didn't mention she heard it in the coffee shop from a five-year-old.

The women at Erma's table were oddly quiet the rest of the night. Their husbands thought they were up to something.

Monday

The morning dawned gray and drippy, a day not at all befitting early summer. Ryan Reilly was clearing off the window table at the café when he saw them: the two grandmothers standing smack in the middle of the park's big grassy area. The only difference was, they were holding umbrellas instead of wearing sun hats.

Well, that would have been the only difference, if it weren't for the other one. This time, standing with the grandmothers were Erma Beans, Madeline Swivet, Leslie Plunkett and his very own mother!

Robin the waitress passed on her way to refill Sue Ann's coffee cup. "Whatcha staring at Ry?" Ryan opened his mouth to answer, but all that came out was a sound like a cat with a hairball.

Dinner was late at the Reilly house, and for the first time Ryan could remember, they missed the news. The meal of leftover parsnips was interrupted by phone calls from every woman his mother knew. Seventeen in all. His father was Not One Bit Pleased.

The same thing happened at the Beans' house. Willie Beans got so hungry waiting for his wife to get off the phone, he made himself a sardine-and-jelly sandwich.

Leslie Plunkett was besieged by women at Melville's Grocery. And Madeline Swivet's doorbell never stopped ringing.

Tuesday

Ryan Reilly had been at work two hours and had not gone near the table by the window. Coffee cups and water glasses had piled up and up until there was hardly any green Formica showing through. Robin knew why.

In the middle of the park's big grassy area were the two grandmothers, Erma Beans, Madeline Swivet, Leslie Plunkett, Mrs. Reilly and *one hundred and six* other women. Standing. Stock. Still.

At 11:37 A.M., Jason P. Mason, a reporter for the local newspaper, scurried through the door of Beever Brothers Café. He ordered a bowl of homemade chicken-and-chickpea soup, which, if truth be told, was not homemade at all, and for the next hour slurped and wrote, slurped and wrote, slurped and wrote.

Ryan and Robin tried to see what he was writing, but every time they came close, Jason covered his notes with his skinny little arm. "You'll see soon enough," he said, dribbling soup down the front of his brown plaid shirt.

They didn't have long to wait. That afternoon, *The Town Trumpet* ran his story on the front page along with a photo of the women taken from the roof of City Hall. Mostly it showed the tops of their heads.

Jason P. Mason, who was not considered a particularly colorful journalist, even by his own mother, must have been inspired by something in the Beever Brothers' soup because the story he wrote was brilliant. At least that's what the men said who gathered at the Coffee Corner in Bumble's Bookstore.

The article poked pitiful fun at women who thought they could save the world—or anything else for that matter—by standing in the park. As for the silly, misguided grandmothers who started it all, best they get back to their knitting.

"The world doesn't need saving," said Murphy Beebell, unofficial leader of the Coffee Corner group. "And if it did, we have armies for that, and elected officials."

"Hear, hear!" said Clyde Cleveland.

"Besides, they're not even carrying banners or shouting slogans," said Duncan Willows. "Everyone knows you can't save the world without banners and slogans."

The men nodded and sighed.

∞

"Well, that's that," said Mayor Pudge with a smiley smirk after reading Jason's article. "No woman will dare show her face in the park now."

And at any other time, in any other place, when the news wasn't bad and the world wasn't askew, that might have been true. But not this time.

Wednesday

By eight o'clock the next morning, squiggle-squeezed into the big grassy area, the rose garden, the playground and the pathway leading to the wading pond were *two thousand two hundred and twenty-three* women and one five-year-old girl.

The mayor was beside himself.

"We'll be a laughingstock," he said to Police Chief Barker-Poles. "Do something. Make them go away."

The police chief thought and thought. The women weren't disturbing the peace. They weren't destroying city property. They weren't even littering.

"Aha!" he said finally. "I've got it!"

He grabbed his purple police-chief megaphone and bellowed at the women, who could have heard him even if he'd whispered. "Ladies, your organization didn't apply for a permit to gather in the park. You will have to disperse immediately."

The women smiled weary smiles. No one budged. Not even a millimeter.

"Make them move *now*," the mayor hissed. "Tell them you'll call the police."

"I *am* the police," the police chief said.

"Excuse me, sir," said one of the grandmothers. "We belong to no organization. We're simply women who have chosen to visit a public park, which is our right to do. Wouldn't you agree?"

Chief Barker-Poles, although not used to being disobeyed, especially when he used his purple police-chief megaphone, was a fair and thoughtful man. He pondered and pondered. "They have a point," he said.

And for the rest of the day the women stood in the park.

Not speaking.

Not looking at squirrels.

Not munching on coconut candy.

Not anything at all.

Thursday

Morning newspapers all over the country carried Jason P. Mason's story about 2,223 women, including the mayor's wife, Vera, standing in the park to save the world. Most of the men who read the article laughed. Most of the women became oddly quiet. Mayor Pudge groaned.

Friday

Network news broadcasts all led with the same story: *In towns and cities across America, hundreds of thousands of women, many of them grandmothers, gathered in public parks, school yards, vacant lots, and on the steps of churches, synagogues, mosques and Buddhist centers. They carried no banners, shouted no slogans and belonged to no organization. When asked why they were gathering, one of the grandmothers said, "We're saving the world." The FBI is investigating.*

Ryan Reilly couldn't help smiling as he ate his parsnips. Neither could his mother.

Saturday

rin Green, anchor of the International Television News Association, was first to break the story: *From Beijing to Baghdad, Cairo to Copenhagen, Jerusalem to Johannesburg, all over the world and in nearly every town in America, tens of millions of women are gathering in public squares, city parks, fields and forests. Many of them are grandmothers. They carry no banners, shout no slogans, have no leaders and belong to no organization. The gatherings seem to spring up spontaneously and are peaceful in nature. Stay tuned for more on this remarkable unfolding event.*

In an unrelated story: Reports are still coming in from our affiliates, but it would appear there has been no fighting anywhere in the world today.

The Story of the Story

I always carry a pen in my pocket. Rarely any paper, but always a pen. That morning was no different. I was sitting in my favorite spot—a corner table in the café upstairs over Bloomsbury Books in Ashland, Oregon. In front of me was a yellow mug that read *coffee* in thirteen languages and a copy of *The New York Times*.

Lace curtains covered the windows. Sepia-toned photos of someone's grandparents and great-aunts dotted the walls. An antique buffet held coffeepots, silver spoons, a dish of hard candy and a lamp with a fringed silk shade. I loved the place. I loved the saggy armchairs upholstered in gold velour, the coffee table littered with the newspaper sections no one ever reads, the mismatched lamps. All reminiscent of a sweeter, saner, safer time.

Downstairs was Bloomsbury's, with its creaky floors and shelves of books by famous local authors; its resident cat one is warned not to let out; its staff of helpful humans who read the books they sell and know their customers by name.

"Someday I'll move here," I used to say to myself during stopovers on the long drive between Seattle and San Francisco. I'd imagine what it would feel like to be one of the Bloomsbury regulars. To sit with a lap full of books in the brown leather chair snuggled away between the Poetry section and Travel. To visit with friends in the café.

Then, after years of doing other things, going other places, it finally happened. I moved to Ashland.

Thanks to a small inheritance, I had just enough to rent a cottage for twelve months and hunker down to finish the project-of-a-lifetime: A Serious Nonfiction Book I'd been researching for nearly a decade about ancient scrolls buried in the crypt of a medieval cathedral, the contents of which were destined to save the world.

Ashland was ideal because I knew not a single soul, and there would be no distractions. I'd write blissfully, brilliantly for a year, find a publisher, and live out my dotage on royalties and speaking engagements.

A perfect plan. Except for one tiny thing.

Ashland is not like other places. It's magic. And it has an agenda all its own.

No sooner had I moved into my cozy cottage, organized my books and research notes, filled my cupboard with chocolate bars, and positioned my computer to take full advantage of a heart-melting view of the Siskiyou foothills, than every creative thought I had ever thought, or thought of thinking, evaporated. In its place, a big-time, intractable, unbudgeable, woe-is-me writer's block the size of a subcontinent.

The harder I tried to write my Serious Nonfiction Book about scrolls that would save the world, the more blocked I became. I meditated. I stopped eating chocolate. I walked miles and miles every day to clear my brain. Up hills, down hills, and past a wooden church with a red door and pretty stained-glass windows.

I joined a writers' group. I hired a life coach known for her wisdom. Nothing worked. The more blocked I got, the more unhappy I became. The more unhappy I became, the more blocked I got.

Finally, after months of witless, fruitless striving, I gave up.

"I have stopped trying to push the river," I announced to the very wise life coach. "No longer am I a writer of Serious Nonfiction about scrolls that will save the world."

"In that case," she said, "I know a person who needs healing. Perhaps you can help her. She goes to the wooden church with the red door and pretty stained-glass windows."

I brightened just a bit, for I'd forgotten I am also a healer of persons who need healing. "It is precisely what I will do," I said.

And that's when the magic started.

The more healing I did, the happier I became. The happier I became, the more people came to me for healing. A beautiful young woman whose mother lived in Ashland came all the way from another state. Because I had enough to live on for the year, I asked people to pay me in hugs instead of money. And so they did. Except for a woman who gave me an envelope and said, "Save this for something special."

Life was wonderful. I smiled and smiled.

On a sunny spring morning, I walked into the wooden church with the red door to see from the inside the pretty stained-glass windows. "Hello," a cheerful woman said. "I know everyone in town and I will introduce you. Soon your days will be filled with friends and laughter." And so they were.

One of the people the cheerful woman introduced me to had a terrible, horrible pain in her back. "If you help me, I will tell you something important," she said. It is, at least, what she would have said if she'd known she was about to do that very thing.

So I put my hands on her terrible, horrible pain and she said, "You need to write a children's book for grown-ups."

My heart sank. "I don't write children's books for grown-ups," I said. "I write Serious Nonfiction."

"Toodle-dee-doo," she said. And that was that.

Except, as we all know, it wasn't.

A few days later, the most wonderful something happened. I became a grandmother.

The baby was a girl, and her parents named her Laila. What, I wondered, could I give Baby Laila that would be so especially special she would always remember she had a grandmother who loved her?

"A star!" I thought. "I could have a star named after her."

"There are billions and billions of stars," Laila's father said. "That's not special."

"A chair!" I said. "I could paint a chair with fairies

and dragonflies and a princess crown and her very own name."

"She's too small for a chair now," said Laila's mother. "And soon she'll be too big for it."

I thought and thought.

I could write her a story! But not a children's story because soon she'd outgrow it. And not a grown-up story because she'd have to wait too long to read it. A children's story for grown-ups.

"Toodle-dee-doo," said the woman who used to have a terrible, horrible pain in her back.

Which, in a roundabout way, because that's how things happen in Ashland, brings us right back to where we started: the café upstairs over Bloomsbury Books.

☙

I sipped the last of my coffee from the yellow mug and leafed through *The New York Times*. The news was dreadful.

Fighting in Iraq. Fighting in Afghanistan. Fighting in

Uzbekistan, Sudan, Spain, Haiti, Colombia, Chechnya, the West Bank and Gaza. North Korea and Iran were making scary noises. India and Pakistan were at it again. It was five months before the crabbiest presidential election anyone could remember. The dollar was low. The stock market was low. And the term *French fries* had become an anathema.

In short, the world was askew and getting askewer every day.

"There *must* be a better way," I said to the empty chair across from me.

And in that instant—perhaps because Ashland is magic, but maybe just because it was time—I remembered something a Native American elder said to me a very long time ago: "Men have taken the world as far as they can. It's up to the women to lead us the rest of the way."

I closed the newspaper, smoothed out my napkin, took the pen from my pocket, and with just a hint of sadness, mixed with just a hint of hope, I wrote: "On a buffety, blustery early summer day, when the news was bad and the sky turned yellow, a strange thing happened in the town where I live."

"What's this?" I asked the photo of Great-aunt Somebody on the wall next to me. "And where's it going?"

I didn't have long to wait.

"That morning, two grandmothers who had never met, not even by accident, put on their summer Sunday clothes, their most comfortable shoes, their favorite sun hats, and walked to the park in the center of town."

Having run out of napkin space, I said good-bye to the café owner and walked up the street to the cottage wherein languished my unused computer. A few words hastily scribbled on a paper napkin and *The Great Silent Grandmother Gathering* was born.

∞

"Yoo-hoo!" they called from a stone bench in front of the town fountain. It was the beautiful young woman from another state who had come to me for healing. With her was her mother.

"Let me read you the story I wrote for my granddaughter," I said as we sat in the sun drinking tea.

When I finished, the mother said, "I'm going to a Very Big Conference. I must take copies of your story."

"But it's just a little story for my granddaughter."

"A hundred copies would be good," the mother said.

"Maybe it could be a little booklet," said her beautiful daughter.

"We might need two hundred copies," the mother said.

"With artwork," said her beautiful daughter.

"But it's just . . . "

"Perhaps we should have it translated," the mother said. "Hebrew, Arabic and French. It is, after all, going to the United Nations."

"Ohmyohmyohmy!" I said.

"Let me read you the story I wrote for my granddaughter," I said to the life coach known for her wisdom. "It's going to the United Nations."

"Here," she said when I finished. "You'll need money to print the booklet."

"You'll need art for the cover," another friend said. "Here's a greeting card with art that is perfect. Lots and lots of grandmothers. I'm sure the illustrator will let you use it."

"There's another Very Big Conference coming up," said the mother of the beautiful daughter. "More copies."

"Here," said friends, "you'll need money."

"Let us perform the story," said an actress.

"But it's just a little story for my granddaughter."

"We'll do a splendid job, and you can sell your booklets," she said.

"I have no more booklets."

"Then you'll need to print more," said the cheerful woman who had introduced me to so many people.

"Maybe a woman gave you an envelope to save for something special."

One of the helpful humans from Bloomsbury's phoned, "Would you like to read your story at our store?"

"Ohmyohmyohmy!" I said. "Indeed I would!"

"The radio," a man said. "We want to interview you on the radio about your book."

"It's not a book," I said. "It's just a little story."

"We need more books," said the helpful humans at Bloomsbury's. "A lot more books."

"There's a Very Big Conference on peace," the beautiful young woman's mother said. "This time in South Africa. We need books."

"It's just a booklet," I said. "Not a book."

And so it went. Orders started coming in from around the world. Bookstores in other towns asked for the story. One day the pastor of the wooden church with the red door and pretty stained-glass windows said maybe I'd like to read the story there. I smiled and smiled.

The year passed quickly. I did not finish my project-of-a-lifetime, my Serious Nonfiction Book about buried scrolls that will save the world. All I wrote was a little story for a newborn babe about grandmothers standing in the park. A story that by all rights should have gone utterly unnoticed.

And at any other time, in any other place, when the news wasn't bad and the world wasn't askew, that might have been true. But not this time.

—Sharon Mehdi
December 13, 2004
Ashland, Oregon

It Took a Village

Special thanks to Ellen Anderson, Elizabeth Austin, Jean Bakewell, Nancy Bardos, Ronda Barker, Sheila Burns, Margaret Chiloquin, David Churchman, Victoria Crane-Walker, Kay Cutter, Pam Derby, Deborah Elliott and the Hamazons, Jeff Golden, Marta Gomez, Shirley Grega, Tia Hatch, Keith Henty, Judy Hilyard, Sara Hopkins-Powell, Beth Hyjek, Robin Porter, Sandra Scofield, Emma Sweeney, Donna Tallman, Diana Van Vleck, Heather Wade, the staff at Bloomsbury Books, the folks at Viking, and so many others, especially the women of Southern Oregon who, week after week, quietly and resolutely stand for peace.